This book is inspired by a true story. I had a sweet tooth growing up, and my mother always told me how challenging it was to keep me away from the sweets that she had prepared for guests. So, I decided to retell this childhood story using my two sons as the inspiration for Idu and Adu.

Idu (Ee-doo) is the older brother who's playful and protective and Adu (Aa-doo) is his younger brother, a boisterous brat. Idu and Adu mean "this" and "that" in Kannada, my mother tongue. Kannada is the principal language spoken in Karnataka in the south of India. My hope is that as personal as this story is to me, it's also universal in its appeal and will resonate with all of you.

To Amma and Pappa who saw dreams for me before I could, Vivek for his steadfast support, and Siddharth and Aditya for being my joy in every step I take.

www.mascotbooks.com

10 Gulab Jamuns: Counting with an Indian Sweet Treat

For more information, please contact:
Mascot Books
560 Herndon Parkway #120
Herndon, VA 20170
info@mascotbooks.com

Library of Congress Control Number: 2017908924

CPSIA Code: PRT0817A
ISBN-13: 978-1-68401-261-9

Printed in the United States

10
GULAB JAMUNS

counting with an indian sweet treat

Written by
Sandhya Acharya

Illustrated by
Vanessa Alexandre

Idu and Adu were very excited. They were going to have guests that evening. Dia and Mia were coming over for dinner. Mamma had already cooked many delicious things.

It was time to make something special for dessert: GULAB JAMUNS!

"What are **GULAB JAMUNS?**" asked Idu.

"They are little round sweets that look like donuts," Mamma replied. "They are soaked in sugary syrup so when you bite into one, it melts in your mouth."

"Yummy!" said Idu and Adu together.

Mamma kneaded
the dough.

She divided it into
small balls.

Then she fried
them in ghee.

Next, she made a sugar syrup
and poured it into a bowl.
Then, one by one, she put the golden balls into the bowl.

Idu counted aloud, "1,2,3,4,5,6,7,8,9,10. 10 GULAB JAMUNS!"

"10 GULAB JAMUNS!" Adu repeated.

Mamma put the bowl of GULAB JAMUNS on the table. "These are for the guests," she said. "Don't touch them!" Then she sent the boys off to play and went about her chores.

The boys played together, but couldn't forget about the **GULAB JAMUNS** on the table.

Suddenly, Adu had an idea.

He climbed on the chair, then the table. He reached into the bowl and bit one GULAB JAMUN and swallowed it!

Then, he put one more GULAB JAMUN in his left cheek and another GULAB JAMUN in his right cheek.

Just then, Mamma walked into the kitchen. Adu got down
from the table in a hurry and hid behind his brother.
"Uh-oh," he said.

Mamma looked at the bowl and asked Idu,
"How many **GULAB JAMUNS** did I make?"

"10," said Idu.

"How many **GULAB JAMUNS** do you see in the
bowl now?"

Idu counted aloud, "1,2,3,4,5,6,7.
7 GULAB JAMUNS."

"Swa gua amoons," Adu repeated,
his mouth full.

"What happened to the other three?"
Mamma asked.

"Adu ate them," Idu confessed.

"But how did he eat them?" Mamma asked.

"Like this!" Idu said.

He climbed on the chair, then the table, then he reached into the bowl. He bit one GULAB JAMUN and swallowed it before putting one GULAB JAMUN in his left cheek and another GULAB JAMUN in his right cheek.

He turned to Mamma and smiled wide.

Mamma laughed. She wiped their sticky hands and faces. "I made 10 GULAB JAMUNS this morning. Adu ate three and Idu ate three. How many GULAB JAMUNS do we have left in the bowl?"

Adu counted. "1,2,3,4. 4 GULAB JAMUNS."

"Four gua amoons,"
Idu repeated, his mouth full.

"4 gulab jamuns left," Mamma said. "One for me, one more for Idu, and one more for Adu."

"But we still have one left," said Idu and Adu together.

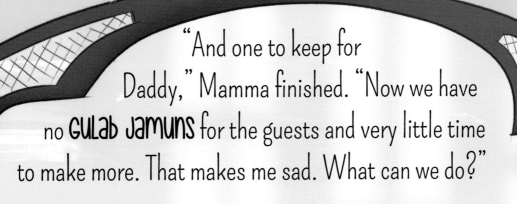

"And one to keep for Daddy," Mamma finished. "Now we have no **GULAB JAMUNS** for the guests and very little time to make more. That makes me sad. What can we do?"

"We will help you make more!" cried Idu and Adu together.

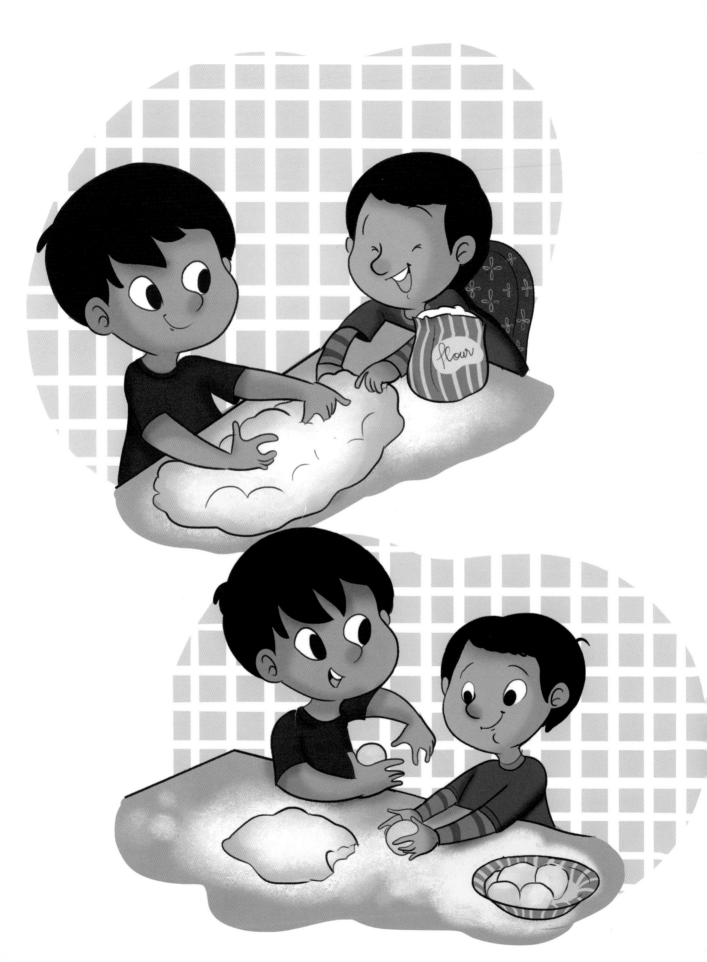

That afternoon, Idu and Adu didn't go to the backyard to play. They helped Mamma and Daddy make 10 more **GULAB JAMUNS** instead!

Before long, Dia, Mia, and their parents were there for dinner.

After dinner, Idu and Adu helped serve the **GULAB JAMUNS** to all the guests. But Idu and Adu didn't want any **GULAB JAMUNS** – they had had enough for the day!

Gulab Jamuns

Prep Time: 10 minutes
Cook Time: 15 minutes

Total Time: 25 minutes
Yield: 10 Gulab Jamuns

ingredients

sugar syrup

- 1 cup water
- 1 1/4 cup sugar
- one 3-4 inch cinnamon stick
- 4-5 cardamom pods
- 10-15 saffron threads
- 1 tsp rose water
- 1/2 tsp lime juice

Dough

- 1/2 cup dry milk powder
- 1 tbsp self-rising flour
- 1 tbsp Bisquick
- pinch of cardamom powder
- pinch of salt
- 2 tbsp warm milk
- 1 tsp ghee

instructions

1. Heat oil to 300°F.

sugar syrup

1. Add water, sugar, cinnamon stick, cardamom seeds, and saffron into a small saucepan. Heat on low heat until all the sugar has melted. Boil for 5 minutes. Add rose water and lime juice. Keep on low heat, slightly simmering.

Dough

1. In a small bowl, add milk powder, self-rising flour, Bisquick, cardamom powder, and salt and mix well. Add warm milk and stir until well incorporated. It will be a wet sticky batter. Add in ghee and stir in. The batter should be sticky but should be easy to shape into a ball.
2. Grease your hands with ghee and take a teaspoon-amount of dough and roll into a ball, making sure there are no cracks! Continue until all the dough is gone.
3. Drop dough into hot oil, it will look like the oil isn't hot enough, but it is! Just give it some time. The dough will slowly rise up. Fry until golden brown (~6-8 minutes). Place the ball into a container. Use a fork to remove the cinnamon and cardamom pods. Pour all the hot syrup over them. Set aside to soak for 1-2 hours, preferably overnight. Top with chopped pistachios and almonds!

Gulab Jamun Recipe from Hetal Vasavada

Hetal Vasavada is a recipe developer and food photographer based out of San Francisco. She is a former MasterChef™ contestant and has worked as a recipe writer over the past three years. She has a passion for food, family, and travel. You can find more of her recipes on her blog at milkandcardamom.com.

About the Author

Sandhya Acharya grew up in Mumbai, India, and now lives in Santa Clara, California. She has always loved eating Gulab Jamuns, though she must confess she may not be great at cooking them. She does love cooking stories though. When she is not writing, she is busy training for marathons, learning a form of Indian classical dance, and enjoying the childhood of her young sons. She won third prize in the 2017 Katha Fiction Contest, which was co-hosted by India Currents and the Wellstone Center, and she blogs regularly at www.sandhyaacharya.com.

Sandhya Acharya

Have a book idea?

Contact us at:

info@mascotbooks.com | www.mascotbooks.com